DON'T GET DIRTY GERTY

For Jenny with love – ED

For Rich – LC

For Clare on her 5th birthday,

Love

Elizabeth Dale

(Aunty Jane)

First published in Great Britain in 1997
Bloomsbury Publishing Plc, 38 Soho Square, London W1V 5DF

Copyright © Text Elizabeth Dale 1997
Copyright © Illustrations Louise Comfort 1997
Art Direction Lisa Coombes

The moral right of the author and illustrator has been asserted
A CIP catalogue record of this book is available from the
British Library

ISBN 0 7475 3046 7

Printed by Bath Press, Great Britain

10 9 8 7 6 5 4 3 2 1

Little Readers

DON'T GET DIRTY GERTY

Elizabeth Dale

Pictures by Louise Comfort

Bloomsbury Children's Books

Gerty was very excited. She was going to Jenny's party that afternoon. On the way, she and her mum were picking up all her friends.

At last it was time to put on her new dress.

She looked so pretty, so clean.
In fact, quite unlike Gerty at all!
"Don't get dirty, Gerty!" cried her mum
as they left.
Gerty slammed the door so hard, the
whole house shook!

While Mum waited in the car, Gerty called for James. He was cleaning his teeth, which took a very long time!

"Have some slime juice while you wait, Gerty," said James's mum.

Next, they went to pick up Harry.

Harry was helping his mum mix a chocolate sludge cake.

Gerty didn't touch the mixture, but she bumped
into the table, sending the bowl flying!

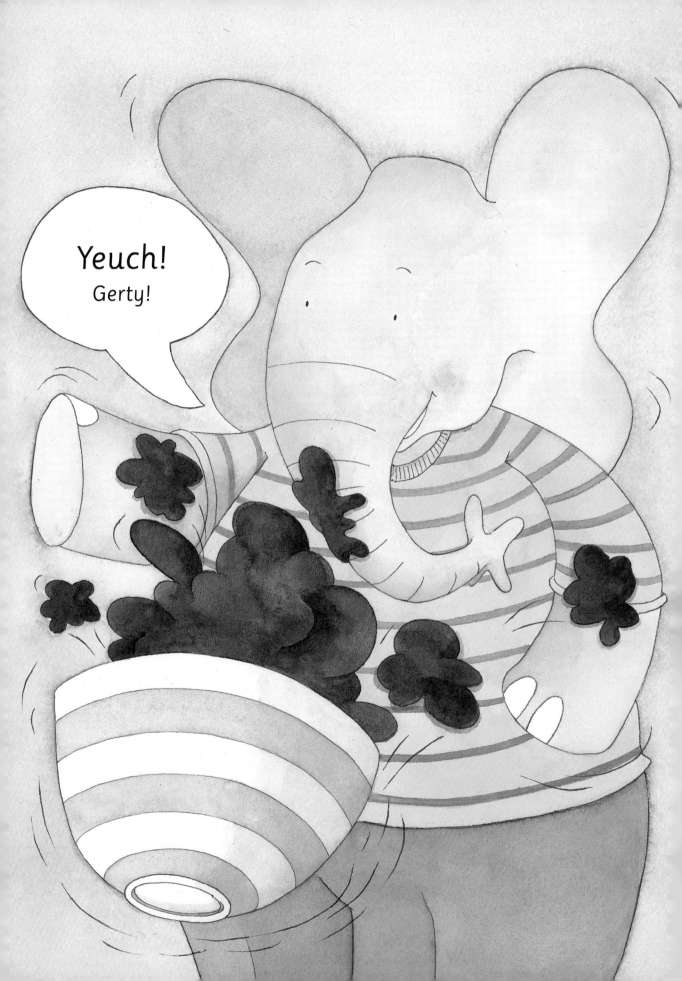

Then they arrived at Mandy's house.

Mandy and her mum were sharing a plate of crunchy ants.

Some ants crawled up Gerty's leg. She jumped up and down and crashed into Mandy.

After that they went to collect Simon.

Simon was snoozing in a hammock.

She shook the hammock to wake him up.

Then they went to pick up Tommy.

Don't get dirty, Gerty!

Tommy was painting the bird table.

Gerty didn't touch the wet paint, but she knocked over the paint-pot.

The last friend to collect was Susie.

Susie's mum was watering the garden.

Gerty didn't realise she was standing on the hose pipe.

At 4 o'clock they all arrived at the party.
"Right on time!" said Gerty. "And I didn't
even get dirty, Mum."

"No! But look at your friends," said Gerty's mum.

"Hello! I'm glad you could all come!" cried Jenny's mum. "And how clever of you to wear your scruffy clothes . . .